# Parrots
## of the
# Caribbean

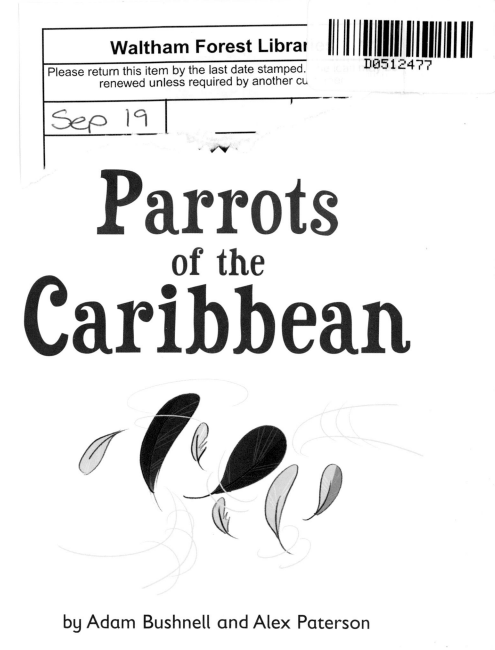

## by Adam Bushnell and Alex Paterson

### W
### FRANKLIN WATTS

# Chapter 1

Once, on a faraway island in the Caribbean, there lived a terrible sea-monster. It had the head of a shark, the body of an electric eel and the claws of a crab. This sea-monster loved nothing more than to eat people. It would slide silently on to land in the dead of night to catch its prey and then slither away again as silently as it had come.

3

It took the people it caught back to its lair
and locked them in a silver cage until
it was hungry.

Then there would be a **munch** ...

and a **crunch** ...

and they were gone!

Stories of the strange-looking monster spread far and wide across the kingdom and, although few people had ever seen it, everyone was afraid of the terrible creature.

One dark night, the monster began to feel hungry again. The silver cage was empty so the monster slid under the surface of the sea and swam towards land. Spotting the royal palace jutting out, not far from the water's edge, it slithered over the sand and up the high walls.

It slipped in through an open window and captured the sleeping prince. Before the young prince could shout for help, the sea-monster had grabbed him and slid quickly back to the sea. It disappeared under the waves without so much as a splash.

# Chapter 2

The next morning, when everyone realised

the prince was missing, there was great panic.

"What will we do?" cried the king.

"Who will find our boy?" sobbed the queen.


Then Sasha, the prince's nanny, stepped forward.

"I know who will help," she said. "The Parrots

of the Caribbean will!"

Everyone turned to look at her.

"Who?" they all gasped

Then from a distance came the sound of flapping.

It came nearer ... and nearer ... and grew louder

and louder!  There was a flutter of feathers, then

in an explosion of colour, four parrots burst

through the open window and into the palace.

"They're here!" Sasha gasped. "The Parrots

of the Caribbean have answered our call!"

13

The super fast parrot led the team as they sped over the sea. Suddenly, they caught sight of a dark, mysterious island. The water reflected the dark, ominous clouds above. As the parrots neared the island, the water swirled and the waves grew to the size of mountains which thrashed and bashed against one another.

Below the gnarled and jagged rocks, the parrots could make out a deep, dark cave. The super fast parrot got there first but the entrance was blocked by a huge boulder. The strong parrot stepped forward. With two punches of its wings, the boulder was reduced to dust.

The extremely strong parrot pointed to its back and the prince jumped on. The parrots sped over the stormy water, back towards the palace. When they reached the beach, the prince jumped down off the back of the strong parrot, relieved.

Just then the parrot with super hearing cupped its feathers around its head. It squawked and pointed across the sea. The sea-monster had woken and was coming this way!

The sea monster fell to the ground ... dead.

The extremely strong parrot rolled the boulder to one side. The sea-monster lay flat on its back, not moving. But to the parrots' horror, the boulder that had crushed the sea monster had also squashed the prince!

Was he alive? Was he breathing?

The parrot with the beautiful voice stepped forward.

The three parrots held their breath as the fourth parrot opened its beak and began to sing ... Its song was so beautiful that the prince slowly started to murmur. Then he sat up. Then he stood up. He was alive! The parrots all squawked with joy. Happily, they set off toward the palace with the prince.

The king and queen were delighted. They threw a party to celebrate the prince's safe return. The parrots proudly told the guests the story of their daring rescue. The king presented each of the parrots with medals for their bravery.

Meanwhile, far across the sea, something was stirring. When the singing parrot had sung his magical song, it had brought the prince back to life … but it had also reawakened the sea-monster! Slowly, it slithered into the water and swam back toward its island in the sea. There was no doubt he would be meeting the Parrots of the Caribbean again one day …